STORYTIME   B

This book is due for return on or before the last date shown
above: it may, subject to the book not being reserved by
another reader, be renewed by personal application, post, or
telephone, quoting this date and details of the book.

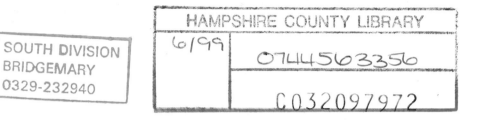
First published 1993 by Walker Books Ltd
87 Vauxhall Walk, London SE11 5HJ

This edition published 1999

2 4 6 8 10 9 7 5 3

© 1993 Jez Alborough

Printed in Hong Kong

British Library Cataloguing in Publication Data
A catalogue record for this book is
available from the British Library.

ISBN 0-7445-6335-6

HIDE AND SEEK

Jez Alborough

WALKER BOOKS
AND SUBSIDIARIES
LONDON • BOSTON • SYDNEY

I'm Frog.
I'm playing hide and seek
with my friends,

but I can't see anyone.
Can you?

I'm playing hide and seek
with my friends,

but Hippo and I
can't see anyone.
Can you?

I'm playing hide and seek
with my friends,

but Hippo, Snake and I
can't see anyone.
Can you?

I'm playing hide and seek
with my friends,

but Hippo, Snake, Tortoise
and I can't see anyone.
Can you?

I'm playing hide and seek
with my friends,

but Hippo, Snake, Tortoise, Toucan and I can't see anyone. Can you?

Now where's Frog?
We can't see him anywhere.
Can you?

MORE WALKER PAPERBACKS
For You to Enjoy

Some more Flip the Flap Books

WASHING LINE
by Jez Alborough

Whose are those stripy socks, that tiny dress, those enormous
underpants, hanging on the washing line?
Which animals do they belong to?
Flip the flaps and see!

0-7445-6309-7   £3.99

TICKLE MONSTER
by Paul Rogers/Jo Burroughes

If you're ticklish, you'd better watch out – the tickle monster's about!
He'll tickle you here, he'll tickle you there; he'll tickle you everywhere!

0-7445-6310-0   £3.99

SPOOKY HOO-HAA!
by Tony Mitton/Daniel Postgate

There are no such things as witches, vampires, ghosts or monsters,
are there? That's just spooky hoo-haa, isn't it? *Or is it?*
Flip the flaps for some shivery surprises!

0-7445-5714-3   £3.99